The Sword of Jasmine

As told by Jason   part 2
Angelica

Patricia Marie G

Author Patricia Marie G
Visit my website at https://www.keytothegatellc.com/
Printed in the United States of America

First Printing: 2018
Key To The Gate LLC
ISBN-13 978-1-7321395-8-9

Contents

Chapter One

Jason and six young warriors

Jason walked towards the sitting room. His excitement put a dance to his step. His body freely kept step to the tune he whistled.

His face lit up with a smile.

He is such a delightful sight to watch.

Under his arm, Jason carried his trusted companion and friend, his old worn blanket.

He looked forward to his time by the warm fire.

He said, "oh yes now I can again daydream about my years of long ago. Such a glorious, blessed day."

This is his second day at the inn.

His hopes are to enjoy his story with an audience.

He thought I do so hope to find someone to share my tales with especially those six young warriors.

They were quite surprised by this old warrior. Yes, indeed they were surprised.

Jason said," yes indeed this a good day to delight myself with precious memories. I will enjoy this." He laughed with pure joy.

He arrived at the sitting room only to find the six arrogant young warriors waiting for him.

He laughed with pleasure to see the warriors.

Jason in his arrogant way said to the six warriors; "I see it is again my destiny to amuse both you and myself."

Jason laughed at the joy of again destiny allowed him an audience.

Jason said," the importance of this old man seems to grow with each story I tell you. My stories are truly wonderful to me and apparently you also."

Jason said, "I truly have lived a magnificent life."

They all laughed as they remembered their first meeting with Jason.

One of the six asked, "Jason your Queen was just kidding us when she said, "she was deciding if she should spare our life because of you. I am right she was playing?"

Jason answered, "Oh no, she was not kidding. Give thanks you only heard of the Sword Of Jasmine. She is swift and accurate with her sword when it involves me."

Preston asked, "Jason is it a sword or a legend of her use of her sword?"

Jason answered, "it is both Preston."

Samuel quickly spoke, "the sword we saw upon her side is that the Sword of Jasmine?"

Jason answered, "yes it is her father's sword. It is the famous Sword of Jasmine."

"It is the same sword formed from the jewels Queen Julia received from King James. She gave me her jewels for the sword. I took them to the swords creator. He created the wedding sword given to King James by her."

"Truly a magnificent sword isn't it?"

Preston said, "so it is the sword she lifted up after using it to defeat Jabel in your first story."

"She sure seems to love you."

Jason smiled as he replied, "I told you how the beautiful, fine ladies love me."

"She is only one of many beautiful Queens who love me."

His arrogance made the six warriors shake their heads and laugh.

Roy one of the six said, "you are so arrogant. Do you realize you said, Queens?"

Jason replied, "Roy I know well what I said. I am rightfully a little well maybe a lot arrogant. I have earned the right to be."

Jason said, "from the sounds of your laughter, you are already amused."

"I think you are now delighted in my destiny and yours of being snowed in together. And you did not think I was going to be important" He smiled feeling very happy.

Preston said, "we came early today as to not wake you. We thought you would tell us more about your story. "

He added. "if you have one left to tell?"

Jason laughed and said, "I always have more of the story to tell. A lifetime of them to tell."

Samuel asked, "how did you have so many beautiful women in your life?"

Jason answered, "yes; I sure have loved and cared for some beautiful women. Such glorious pleasure they gave me in life."

Jason sighed with joyous thoughts than laughed.

He said, "I am blessed with great skill in avoiding the cold-hearted women. Yes, indeed they never caught me. Some came close, but I proved to be too swift and clever for them."

Jason said; "let me get my precious old friend, my blanket just right. I will then tell you an amazing true story."

Several of the men shook their head as they watched Jason. He was so involved in placing the blanket upon himself.

One of the six, Clay asked, "Jason why do you not carry a nice new blanket? The Queen you travel with would get you any blanket you wanted."

Jason's humorous expression turned serious as he held his arms over his chest hugging the blanket against himself.

He answered, "like me, this blanket has had a delightful life. This old blanket is as dear to me as a golden fleece.

Jason paused for a minute then said, "well even more valuable this gives warmth and gold can be so very cold as it flees from the hand."

"It has been with me during times of overpowering joy. "

"This blanket was given to me by a mighty king, King James."

"The painful tears of a Queen fell upon it. There is none that can replace this blanket."

"I placed it on the shoulders of his queen, Queen Julia when we fled for safety."

Andrew one of the six men asked, "when you fled with Queen Julia while King James fought evil Jabel?"

Jason answered, "yes Andrew. It was at the same time. Such a horrible time of terror."

"I wrapped it around his daughter, Jasmine after her birth."

"I laid it over her when Jasmine was ill coming out of battle. I left her and went for help, knowing this blanket would keep her warm until my return."

Samuel said, "that is when Jasmine and Jeffrey fell in love."

Jason smiled as he thought of Jasmine's and Jeffrey's love story.

He happily replied, "They fell in love a long time before that time."

"Yes, she sure took hold of his heart."

"I wrapped up their baby girl after her birth."

Preston thinking out loud whispered, "so Angelica is Jasmine's daughter."

Jason was caught up in his story he did not hear Preston. He continued his tale.

"I placed it upon myself in–between those amazing times of life.

This blanket is my old friend and companion. When I wrap up in it, my memories have become so sweet to me."

Roy, one of the young men, asked, "what about Angelica you spoke of?"

Jason laughed and answered, "that is right I have yet to tell you of Angelica or Heather."

Jason leaned back and smiled; "Angelica was more of a handful than even her mother, Jasmine. Oh yes indeed."

The six young men smiled, sighed as they also leaned back.

Jason said, "as her mother Angelica was fearless."

"Jasmine loved the land. As for Angelica, she loves the open seas."

Preston asked, "how much of these stories are true."

Jason laughed. He said, "enough to amuse us both. You have met my amazing Queen Jasmine and seen the sword on her side. Yes indeed."

"Lean back and enjoy this glorious journey."

Jason added, "Angelica is the heir to the throne of Jasmine. She is a royal princess upon this earth. Her destiny was to be the Queen of the seas."

"She is the soul mate to the king of the seas. The seas and everything else knew the fire between Angelica and the king was too great to be put out. The seas also knew Angelica, and her king was born to rule over them."

"Men, I tell you their love brightened the stars in heaven."

Samuel said, "a King and Queen of the seas love story."

Jason said, "yes Samuel. I think it best men to begin by telling you of Princess Angelica and how her destiny led her to become the Queen of the seas."

"She was a delightful child."

"Angelica, Queen Jasmine's beautiful baby girl. Trust me; the baby girl was healthy with great lungs. Oh, my was she ever born with a warrior's shout. She still commands attention."

Jason looked very serious and with a gesture said, "but of course, she loves me enough to let me get away with just about anything."

The six warriors laughed at Jason's statement.

"King Jeffrey lifted the baby girl up and said, "you are sent from heaven sealing mine, and your mother's love."

"I name you, Princess Angelica."

Jason laughed as he said; "I do think there were times King Jeffrey wondered if he had correctly named her."

"Yes, indeed she gave him a challenge."

"He is kind, with an understanding love for the ladies in his life."

Queen Julia said, "God has truly touched him with a patient, loving nature."

"God knew Jeffrey also would need a brave spirit."

"I highly agreed with her."

"I have seen with my own eyes Jeffrey willing to fight at Jasmine's side no matter the odds. He rode and stood strong."

"He was also a major factor to her reaching her destiny and regain her father's kingdom."

"Many times, I watched him risk his life to intercept the enemy keeping her safe."

Preston commented, "that creates a great king and unity."

"King Jeffrey became king due to love and his bravery."

Jason replied, "yes Preston that is true. Yes, a great man and king."

"Only a brave man can love a woman in such an amazing way yet fear no enemy he could face."

Samuel replied, "only a powerful love and bravery."

"He rode in front at her side against the armies of Jabel. Is that right?"

Jason knotted his head as he answered,"yes Samuel he rode at Jasmine's side against Jabel and his wicked family."

"He never hesitated, nor did he fall back."

"He helped me fight against the odds to give her the freedom to fight Jabel one on one. We all knew it was her destiny to defeat Jabel."

Roy said, "it's sad he didn't believe his love was enough to reign at her side. To believe another was more kingly to reign with her is so sad. To think another man would."

Jason said,"No, he never felt he would reign at her side."

"His love for her and her future was strong enough to surrender unto what her destiny was."

Roy said, "I would find it hard to love like that."

Jason answered, "Of course I have loved with every minute of the day many brave, beautiful women."

"My love was different than their love, but I surrendered to love like that."

Preston asked, "Jason you never married to ensure you could stay at Queen Julia's side. Do you mean Queen Julia as the one you loved but did get to love that way?"

Jason answered, "Preston our love was as a brother and sister. I always knew mine, and her love is deep in our heart for King James. To this day he alone owns her heart."

"As for Jasmine and Jeffrey. Destiny placed in Jasmine's heart love for him."

"She knew he was to reign with her."

"She never felt he was not her equal due to not coming from a royal bloodline. She believed him a Godly man therefore of a royal lineage."

"Love truly chooses it's lovers without reasoning as to if they both move in the same level of title. Queen Julia was a slave girl and James a mighty King."

Samuel looked down as he said, "it is good their love was not one-sided as mine was."

Jason looked sad as he commented on Samuel' statement, "I am sorry to hear that Samuel."

"Yes, love can make life feel glorious or make someone feel their heart is being ripped out. Such a bad love can make a good love amazing."

Samuel said, "that is true for I do love my next love with greater joy than maybe I would have."

Chapter Two

Angelica

Jason said, "now on to their daughter Angelica."

"She grew gaining strength and beauty. She was told many stories of wisdom and correct judgment."

"Of course, I was her teacher. Yes, indeed they knew I was the best to do such teaching."

One of the six said, "you have such an ego Jason."

Jason responded, "oh be careful. Jasmine being a great warrior and Queen can approach us without us being aware until she firmly makes her presence known."

Preston said, "careful his Queen spoke stern with authority concerning him."

Jason replied, "yes she can sneak up on us. She's a little sneaky."

Jason looked very serious at the warriors as he said, "Now concerning Angelica. Even with her bold nature Angelica's strongest traits were compassion and a tender heart."

"One summer afternoon after Angelica finished her studies; she requested a trip to the marketplace."

"Angelica, myself and her guards set out on the journey."

"Less than a half hour after we arrived, she saw a little girl, hungry and in filthy rags.

The little girl was the same age as Angelica."

"Angelica's eyes filled with tears as she stood still watching the little girl begging food."

"Angelica looked over at me and said, "there shall be no hungry children in my kingdom."

"My mother and father do not know of this hungry girl. I will tell them of this problem. I know where their heart is touched in such matters."

She walked over took the little girl by the hand.

"She told her, "I am Angelica. I am your friend. What is your name?"

The little girl answered, "Heather."

She told Heather, "come with me now."

"She bought Heather garments and food."

"Thus, Angelica and Heather's lifetime friendship began."

"Each time we went to the marketplace, we knew where our first stop would be."

"Angelica and her little friend Heather would laugh and play as they bought goods."

"Angelica needed no training in how to carry herself or capture a heart with her smile. I have not seen a heart able to resist her even until now."

"She was trained in the skills of the sword and the strategy of battle. She was also trained in the knowledge of a healer."

"She was more drawn to watching the movement of water. She loved the currents and tides that rushed upon her feet."

Jason in deep thought said, "children tend to enjoy simple things. The simple things that adults foolishly only pass by paying no attention to at all."

"I can still see her laughing and dancing around chasing the waves of the tide."

"Angelica could have anything she desired yet her great joy cost nothing. I do believe times as those truly can be the most joyous. Such times do lay easy on the mind."

One day Angelica walked from the shoreline to where I was with a sad look on her face.

I asked her, "Angelica what is troubling you?"

She answered, "I was walking on the shoreline leaving my footprints in the sand. The tide came in and washed my footprints away."

"Jason, it was as if I never walked upon the sand. I thought one day will there be something wipe away my life and footprints, as if I never lived?"

I answered her, "I promise you Angelica; you will live on. The footprints of your life already appeared in your concern for the hungry and poor."

Angelica said, "yes it troubles me to see any hungry and poor."

Jason continued, "Because of the compassion in your heart, your mother and father set up a way to care better for the poor children. Does not the less fortunate get fed and clothed without you standing there? Yet, it was your heart that left footprints there."

Angelica answered, "yes they do my dear friend."

Jason continued," Your touch and kindness in Heather's life, does it not live without you standing there? There is no tide strong enough to wash such footprints away. Angelica the whole truth is your footprints' lifespan is determined by where and how you place the footprints of your life."

She smiled and said, "your right my dear friend. I now understand."

She added, "I do so delight in having such a wise yet clever friend."

She always hastened to the shoreline. She would immediately look at her reflection in the water. Each time she saw her reflection, she would say, "I shall rule over you, just as I see my face above you now."

Leaves or anything floating upon the water fascinated her for hours.

King Jeffrey had toy ships made for her to send out to sea and amuse herself.

She did as the shipbuilders instructed her. She carefully named each of her ships. She had their names wrote upon them, with a record of each kept.

Angelica's guards did not find it amusing when Angelica commanded them to recapture her boats from the winds control.

She awarded each of them for their bravery battling the wind. It was a good thing she had them kneel before her as she honored them.

I honestly do not feel they could've stood. The expressions on their faces showed the tremble they felt.

She had watched her parents honor warriors for bravery. She drew her sword laid it flat on each of their shoulders. She joyfully would say, "I Princess Angelica honor you for your bravery."

I must admit I laughed until my sides hurt watching it all. I still find great joy as I remember it.

Angelica would lie upon the grass and watch the birds in flight, and the way tree branches move in the wind.

The way the wind blew Angelica's toy ships as if it controlled them instead of her, did not please her. Far too many of her toy ships were blown away from her view.

She asked me, "Why is the wind both beautiful and mean? How can something be so wonderful causing the trees and flowers to dance as it passes by be so mean also?"

I answered her, "It does seem to have the nature of people sometimes. Like your ships, the trees choose to move with and not against the wind."

After this being a continuous problem for her, she decided to conquer it.

Like her mother Jasmine, Angelica believed nothing was beyond her abilities.

She was lying on the grass in the early morning. She could not take her mind off the wind and how to rule over it.

I came walking up to teach her the morning lesson.

She looked up at me and said, "look up at the clouds. What moves them?"

I answered her, "the wind in heaven."

She looked serious at me and said, "Jason, the wind is mighty. I will conquer it."

I told her, "since God created it then it must remain under his command. You can learn to direct, or use it as you need it."

She replied, "I am sure He will help me learn to prevent its meanness of capturing my ships."

She rose to a sitting position and looked very serious at me.

She asked me, "Jason, my mother is the queen of this mighty land. What will I be the queen of or do?"

I took her by the hand. I asked her, "please walk with me down to the shoreline."

The child's questions keep my mind alert and seeking wisdom. I know my response is important to help form her thinking.

I am careful in such matters because I know the words and actions also affect the future.

I told Angelica, "Touch the water and watch the ripple. When you or your words touch one person's life, it ripples. One of your most important things to remember is, the waters' ripple ends but your touch does not."

"Be careful if your words heal or break lives. Reign with an honorable heart and wise laws. Touch the water again. It did not ripple the same twice nor will your words touch the lives of everyone the same."

Angelica with a serious look on her sweet face said, "I will forever remember those words dear friend Jason."

Chapter Three

Skirts for her fleet of ships

Angelica and I tried to rise to our feet. The wind rose with us.

The long skirt on Angelica was blowing in the wind. She took hold of it on each side and held it out. The wind was slowed down.

Angelica in pure joy said, "Jason my skirt holds back the wind."

I started to agree when Angelica shouted to her guards; "quick men put skirts on my ships. My ships will control the wind instead of the wind capturing my ships."

Angelica laughed and twirled around as she said, "Yes, I have outwitted the wind. The wind will now be my servant. I will wisely command the wind to do as I choose."

I laughed at the expressions on the guard's faces. Both guards looked at each other amazed at Angelica's command.

She commanded, "this is your matter to attend to, quickly warriors. We can now spare many ships in my fleet from loss."

She placed her hands on her hips, raised her little regal head up and commanded, "quick warriors before the wind slows down and goes into hiding from us."

Angelica said, "my mother reigns over the mighty land. I will reign over the wind and the seas."

I laughed, still watching the guards trying to figure out how to put skirts on Angelica's ships.

One of Angelica's guards replied to my laughter, "Jason do not amuse yourself with our dilemma."

The guard's words only increased my laughter.

Queen Jasmine and King Jeffrey came walking up.

King Jeffrey asked, "Jason why are you laughing so?"

I answered him; "Angelica has outwitted the wind."

Angelica spoke up, "mother, father, you will be pleased to know I now reign over the wind. With clever skill, I have learned a way to capture the wind. I commanded my brave warriors to place skirts upon my ships."

Queen Jasmine looked at me and said, in a stern voice, "Jason."

Angelica spoke up, "mother I have learned this on my own."

King Jeffrey looked over at the frustrated guards and said, "Angelica, this is good, but this is work for the shipbuilders. Your guards do not know the ways of shipbuilding."

She replied, "then father let us hurry to those who do know such knowledge. I will have my whole fleet of ships corrected."

Queen Jasmine said, "First Angelica withdraw your command to your guards."

She looked over at her guards and said, "I princess Angelica withdraw my command."

I laughed when the guards said, "long live our King and Queen."

I was turning to return home when I saw a small ship out in our waters.

Queen Jasmine said, "look the ship has the shield of King Charles upon it."

My mother and King Charles have arrived.

Queen Jasmine was very disappointed when she learned it was a messenger.

Instead of King Charles and Queen Julia, a messenger came to us.

He brought word King Charles became very seriously ill two weeks ago.

Queen Julia was staying by his side.

She sent her regrets that she was unable to spend some time with us as expected.

King Charles did not appear for the morning meal. She became very concerned. She sent a servant to find out if he was on his way to eat.

He was trying to get out of bed, only to find himself too weak to do so.

He has made some improvement, yet he is unable to take a long journey.

His improvement was advanced by Kyle and Marie's news to him.

I also delight in such wonderful news. Queen Julia added, "Kyle and Marie have fallen in love."

"The laughter and wedding plans have brought great joy to Kyle's Grandfather."

"The wedding plans which they have set aside until King Charles' recovery."

Queen Julia added, "I hope we will soon be with you. My love is with you without end."

Queen Jasmine was very concerned. She held great respect and felt a deep friendship with King Charles. His kindness and alliance had helped her regain her kingdom.

Time passed with Angelica still commanding her guards. She also commanded her ships with grand acts of authority.

One day her and her guards appeared before her parents. She wanted it official.

Her parents honored her request as they tried not to laugh out loud.

I had a terrible time to keep from laughing.

She had herself announced before she entered.

She said, I Princess Angelica request a larger sword and larger ships. I feel as I grow so should my sword and ships.

King Jeffrey and Queen Jasmine smiled. King Jeffrey replied, "the Queen and myself need a few minutes to consider this important matter."

They looked at each other, and Queen Jasmine said, "we find your request a worthy request, and it is hereby granted, Princess."

Even unto this day, I find tremendous happiness in thinking about her and the guards she kept in a great dilemma.

My life is so full of happiness then and now.

Chapter Four

The wedding

We were eating our evening meal when a guard came in and said, "a ship brought a messenger with word from Queen Julia."

We were all, so concern about its news.

Queen Julia wrote, King Charles has recovered. We are all doing well. This is a great joy to us.

We are all celebrating their engagement.

We wish you to come to Kyle and Marie's wedding.

After the wedding, King Charles is to crown Kyle, king in his stead.

Kyle has shown himself ready to reign over the kingdom.

I believe Marie will make a worthy queen. Do not tell them about this part of the plan. King Charles has planned on surprising them. Kyle will truly be unaware of this plan.

King Charles and I hope to return with you for an extended stay."

Queen Julia signed, "I love you with endless love."

Queen Jasmine was so delighted. She immediately made plans for our journey.

The journey was such a joyful and restful time, well for everyone but the ship captain.

Angelica had the ship captain and crew teach her all they knew.

I laughed amused at the task she gave them.

I heard the captain ask, "good Lord where does she get all these questions from? I believe her mind to be filled with endless questions."

"Oh good Lord give us a little rest."

The good Lord answered him because a little rest is all he got. He sure does need to rethink his prayer.

She skillfully kept them busy.

Heather watched Angelica and kept a smile.

I do wonder if the captain speeded up the ship to hasten our landing. I do believe he did so he could have a quiet time.

We arrived at King Charles a day before the wedding.

Queen Julia and King Charles were walking along the shoreline.

What a glorious reunion. We rushed to embrace them.

King Charles had two crowns prepared for the surprise crowning.

The wedding took place in the garden. The flowers in full bloom gave off their fragrance as a fine perfume.

Queen Julia and Queen Jasmine assisted Marie in getting ready.

We heard their laughter. Their joy and ours filled the castle then the courtyard garden.

A special place was arranged for King Charles to perform the crowning ceremony.

A place next to it was arranged for the wedding.

King Charles stood at Kyle's side in front of the priest.

I waited by the door to walk Marie down the aisle.

I took her hand as I looked over at her to tell her, "you are amazingly beautiful."

King Charles told Kyle, "look how glorious. Grandson, your choice is excellent, truly excellent."

Kyle replied, "yes she is magnificent."

Marie and I heard what they said. She looked over at me smiled and winked.

The priest performing the wedding smiled with pleasure.

I saw Kyle's excitement and whispered to Marie, "let's walk very slow and watch Kyle to see how well he handles waiting for you."

Marie answered, "Jason I loved you even when you are teasing."

I laughed as I told her, "maybe I am not teasing."

After we reached the priest, Kyle looked at Marie and said, "Truly God has blessed me with one of His most valuable treasures for He has shared you with me."

Kyle and Marie both spoke their vows from their heart.

When the priest announced they are now, husband and wife, I saw a few tears fall from King Charles eyes.

The wedding was as Marie, simple, yet beautiful.

After the wedding, King Charles raised his hands to quieten the crowd.

King Charles said, "I have an announcement I wish all to hear."

Please follow me to the area I had set up special."

After everyone was present.

King Charles announced, "Queen Julia and I are going on an extended stay to Queen Jasmine and King Jeffreys.

King Charles added, "I choose not to leave my kingdom unwatched or uncared for."

He continued, "bring forth the crowns for the crowning of Kyle as King and Marie as Queen."

Kyle and Marie looked at each other in total surprise.

King Charles called Kyle forth, "come and kneel before me, grandson."

Kyle kneeled before King Charles, bowed his head.

King Charles said, "my grandson, you have proven yourself worthy to wear this crown and set upon the throne of this kingdom."

Kyle still kneeled looked up at his grandfather and said, "I vow upon my life to bring you and your kingdom honor as long as I live."

King Charles placed the crown on Kyles' head and said, "I now crown you, King Kyle over my entire kingdom."

King Charles told Marie, "Marie kneel before me."

Marie kneeled before King Charles.

Marie while still kneeled before King Charles said, "I vow to bring you and your kingdom honor. The heirs I will give life to will also honor you and your kingdom."

King Charles placed the crown on Marie and said, "I crown you, Queen Marie."

Everyone cheered and shouted, "reign without end, King Kyle, and Queen Marie. Power to your throne and reign."

The banquet celebration was amazing filled with joy, wonderful music, and dancing.

I watched with a joyful heart.

Marie and Kyle were dancing, laughing as they filled the room with love. They danced their wedding dance with love and grace.

After their wedding dance, Marie took King Charles's hand.

We all laughed with joyful hearts as she led him to the dance area.

She bowed and asked, "may I have this dance our mighty king?"

King Charles laughed with joy then answered, "I may have forgotten, it has been so long."

King Kyle encouraged his grandfather to dance with Marie.

King Charles smile in pure joy.

He said, "to dance with you will be an honored granddaughter."

Their dance was a delightful event.

A wonderful sight to behold his happiness.

King Kyle and Queen Marie said goodnight.

King Charles looked at us with pleasure.

He said, "remember when you first came here? I lived so alone and broken-hearted. I felt I was being punished with a slow death."

We all said, "yes we remember."

Jasmine said, "it broke my heart to see your sorrow."

He continued, "I have daily watched this miracle forming until today. Now, look at this glorious miracle."

"What a magnificent wedding."

The next morning King Kyle and Queen Marie walked us to the shoreline.

King Kyle's affection and love were no longer awkward.

He embraced his grandfather as he told him, "I love you. Thank you for forgiving me for the times I did not deserve you as my grandfather."

King Charles with tears in his eyes, held Kyle tight and said, "I love you, I always have and always will."

We watched them with a rejoicing heart. We all remember the rebellion and cruelty King Charles suffered from Kyle. Only God can transform someone as Kyle had been.

Chapter Five

Returning Home

We boarded the ship to return home.

The Captain and crew were very ready for Angelica.

The Captain had a stool built for her. He placed it at the helm.

The captain smiled as she boards his ship.

He leaned back with his hands on his side. He gestured to her.

He told her, "This is for you to stand on. I want you to see in front of us."

"I know your commanding nature will again be made evident as it did last time."

She stood on the stool and helped steer the ship home.

She was so happy, laughing and feeling the wind blow through her hair.

The captain was amazed at the natural ability she had at the helm.

Often, I looked over at Queen Julia out of concern.

She was returning home for the first time since we fled to safety.

The closer we came to our home, I knew how more intense her feelings and memories.

I saw Queen Julia standing on the side of our ship staring out to sea.

The memories were so visual as Queen Julia. The memories appeared between the open sea and the heavens. I walked over to her.

As I stepped beside Queen Julia, I must have also stepped into her display of memories.

She said, "you were so young when we first met."

I looked in the direction she was looking. I also visually saw our memories on display before me. Each memory is sweet, precious to our soul.

Soft breezes touched us and blew through our hair.

The movement of the water gently rocked the ship.

One of those times when I asked Queen Julia if she was alright?

She replied, "yes Jason. I was thinking of the time we fled."

"All the years since I have longed in my heart to return home. This is not the way I dreamed of our return for so very many years."

She asked, "Jason is it difficult to be home without our dear King James?"

I answered her, "worst at first and still at times. After all these years, I miss him. I often find myself looking down the path he would come home on."

She said, "I understand many times I thought I saw him riding towards me while I waited for him at the village."

I told her, "yes I often thought I saw him riding to the castle so plain I would start to run greeting him."

Queen Julia with tears in her eyes said, "King James told me our dance would last a lifetime. I answered him a lifetime wouldn't be long enough. We were both correct. No number of lifetimes would be long enough."

I told her, "the amazing love you shared is as no other. The time you had together was far too short but glorious."

She continued "I know my heart will never stop longing for him. My love for him has not decreased over the years. Our love gave us the rhythm of life. I still hear the music of our dance."

I smiled and asked her, "did you ever actually hear music, or did you play along with King James?"

Queen Julia answered me; "I heard the music the minute my eyes first beheld him. King James' presence took hold of my heart."

I told her, "King James told me God showed him you were to be his Queen. You had his heart touched by God from the start."

She said, "really, oh my, if only I knew that. I didn't let him know it until I was sure of his feelings. James was a glorious king. I was a slave girl he delivered out of captivity.

I told her, "in his heart and eyes you were his lady and Queen."

She continued, "I felt what hope did I have of ever being close to him, neither the less to become his Queen. I held back my heart until he opened his to me. Well, Jason, you were there in the garden with us."

I replied, "you both played so many games with each other. You both said so much about love with one look at each other."

She said, "just a look from him made my heart fill with joy."

"The way his eyes looked at me made me feel beautiful."

I told her, "When I was a small boy, you both kept me confused, trying to wonder why

I heard no music. Both of you danced to music no one else heard."

I smiled and said, "but all hearts were affected by the rhythm and music you both danced."

We laughed at our precious memories.

Queen Julia said, "Jason on the night before Jasmine rode off to battle Jabel our King James embraced me."

I replied, "when he came to you as in a dream?"

Queen Julia said, "yes, that night. Our spirits embraced. Jason, when King James arms embraced me, I felt all my sorrows and heaviness leave. My heart and soul again felt his love. My soul and heart danced with such joy because I was again in his arms. I knew then in truth one day I will feel his love forever."

I replied, "I believe that also."

I told Queen Julia, "I always wondered but did not want to shame you by asking about your time in captivity."

Queen Julia replied, "I know it was not to my shame. Jason you and I both have seen those who bow with their body yet in their eyes you see a wicked desire."

"There also are those who shine forth some awesome power of pure goodness, like our King James."

She smiled as she continued, "Jason, King James did not gain my freedom with gold. He gained my freedom with a whip.

That statement captured my attention. I found myself amazed.

I replied, "Queen Julia; King James never carried a whip. What do you mean?"

She replied, "no it was not his whip."

She continued, "I was outside doing my daily tasks when King James and his men rode in."

"King James did not wear his crown but rode as one of his men. I looked up and saw him before me. When my eyes looked into his, I saw such glory through his eyes. I was so completely taken by him. My heart bowed in his presence. My body only followed my heart when I bowed myself before him."

I said, "yes even without his crown he had a kingly presence."

She continued, "When the man that was then my master saw me. He took hold of his whip, shouted with a crude voice as he ran towards me, "back to your tasks and bow only to me."

"I could not rise; my soul would not allow me to do so. There had been others who came to our village, but I felt nothing of their arrival."

"When I beheld King James, it was as in my dreams. King James was the great warrior who would gain my freedom. My capturer only struck me once before King James took hold of the whip."

King James shouted at my capturer, as the king's fury repeatedly struck him, "how dare you strike a woman in my presence. You will now feel the whip upon your own back."

Queen Julia laughed and continued, "When King James finish instructing my capturer on his behavior, he commanded a horse given unto me."

I told her, "our King never tolerated abuse on women and children. Nor would he allow a harmless animal abused."

She continued, "King James offered me refuge from such as this man. I accepted his offer. Only later did I learn he was actually a king."

"I felt him watching me the entire trip to his castle. When he wasn't watching me, I found myself watching him. Thus, the music of our love began and still lives on."

I asked her, "do you still hear the music when you think of King James?"

She smiled and said, "Oh yes Jason I do."

"I felt if everyone knew such love then their life would be given the greatest of gifts."

I told her, "Queen Jasmine reigns with the same wisdom and strength as King James did. She is so much like her Father."

She said, "yes she does reign with a mighty sense of justice and an equal mighty sense of mercy. She is truly an extension of her father."

Queen Julia and I looked over at the commotion.

Angelica was busy trying to instruct one sailor the correct way to handle the sword. Angelica told the sailor, "why even a girl could defeat him."

The sailor should not have challenged her to prove her words.

The sailor found himself on the ground with Angelica sword blade at his throat. Everyone was laughing, which made it worse.

Angelica said to the sailor, "I, Princess Angelica choose to spare your life."

"It is the only honorable thing to do. Arise to your feet."

I laughed when the sailor looked over at his shipmates and said, "I had to let her win, she's the Princess."

Queen Jasmine with a stern voice said; "do not urge Angelica on by finding this amusing."

I looked over at Queen Julia and winked. I returned my attention to Queen Jasmine and said, "yes, my Queen you are correct. Yes indeed."

Queen Jasmine never could help but laugh when I did that.

Queen Julia laughed and said to Queen Jasmine, "does this not bring back memories when you did the same?"

Then we all became very amused remembering Jasmine doing the same.

Our ship arrived in our waters.

The guards assisted Queen Julia and King Charles off the ship.

Queen Julia stopped at the shoreline and took a deep breath.

She reached for my hand to walk with her.

We talked of memories from long ago with laughter.

Angelica walked up the shore to us and said, "come grandmother and see my fleet of ships. Like me, they started out small. They have since grown with a great number."

I laughed and said, "yes, also have Angelica tell you of how she reigns over the wind. Also, have her tell you of her command to have skirts on her fleet of ships by the guards."

Queen Julia laughed and asked, "what do you mean Jason?"

I replied, "just ask. Angelica will tell you all about it. She loves to talk about it all."

Queen Julia returned with Angelica from seeing her fleet of ships.

Angelica went on to her chambers.

Queen Julia looked very serious at me and said, "my goodness Jason the girl does believe she rules over the wind. She also feels since her fleet of ships rides on the water, she also rules the seas."

She laughed and said, "Jasmine is surely being repaid for the wiles of her youth."

We both laughed.

It was beyond words to have Queen Julia home again.

Queen Jasmine gave birth to a baby girl.

I laughed as I told King Jeffrey, "we will need help from God and His mercy for sure if they keep multiplying. There are only two of us and so many of them"

He laughed as he replied, "you are right. No doubt we need the wisdom and strength from God for this task."

King Jeffrey lifted the baby girl up and said; "twice I have been given a gift from heaven. I name you Princess Tricia."

I have been training both Heather and Angelica with the sword.

Heather isn't as good as Angelica, but she is excellent herself. She is a natural with the healing teaching.

Heather stayed at the castle and traveled with Angelica. She was humorous and kind.

Destiny had taken a poor little girl begging food to become a girl living in the castle.

Heather was treated as another daughter by Queen Jasmine and King Jeffrey.

So, in all aspects of things they had three daughters.

King Jeffrey handled it all with kindness. He would smile as he watched their schemes and play.

Angelica kept Heather and herself busy.

Laughter and love filled the castle.

Queen Julia is still caring for King Charles. Her care has brought him back to life. He has regained strength.

She is happy to be home. She told me, "I find the joy living where my precious memories were created. At the same time, it increases my longing for him."

I often saw her stop at the door of hers and King James room. A few times the smile turned to tears.

During the times I saw her tears I rush to her side. I would embrace her and allow her to cry.

I understood how being home was both joy and times of sorrow missing him. With that understanding, I was able to comfort her.

A guard came bringing a message for King Charles.

It was from King Kyle. It read, "I am so excited grandfather I can hardly write this. Marie had a healthy son."

"We named our son, your heir, Charles II."

"We love and miss you."

To have their son named in his honor brought great happiness to King Charles.

The guard told King Charles, "King Kyle and Queen Marie have reigned with great honor to King Charles. His kingdom has prospered."

King Charles sent back the guard with a message. It read, "my heart is filled with happiness. I am honored beyond words to have an heir named after me."

"I am proud of you."

"I love and miss you both."

Happiness filled King Charles, and his health is now good. He often speaks of when he would see his namesake.

We had good times laughing about when we first met Kyle. Mostly we laughed at the stories of what lined him out.

I am sure Queen Julia's healing herbs help heal him. I feel the happiness healed his soul from the years of loneliness.

When we first met him it troubled us his lonely sorrow. He had nothing but a lack of love and no kindness towards him.

I feel the lack of love and laughter is a form of torture. The soul must have both to keep the mind and body healthy.

Monthly messages came with love and respect.

King Charles received the 2nd message from King Kyle; it read, "I miss you grandfather. We set our task every day as we feel you would."

"Your namesake is daily taught of you as the great King you truly are."

"We long to see you again."

"Queen Marie sends her love to you and her family."

"Signed your loving grandson and servant."

The messages filled King Charles with happiness.

I never married, nor do I desire to do so. My life is full of glorious blessings daily. So, I choose not to mess it up. I still must outwit a few ladies. They each make it difficult, but I rise above the challenge. Such a challenge brings my heart great delight.

Long ago Angelica made Heather an honorary Princess. They are as real sisters.

They are now seventeen years old.

Angelica became a young woman far quicker than any of us was ready for it to happen.

She has gone from toy ships to designing major ships.

Her guards remained with her from childhood. They spoke of great relief of no longer being commanded to retrieve her ships.

She designed many ships of various types, flying the kingdom flag.

Her pride and joy she calls, the comfort ship.

It was a magnificent ship with carved details.

Her parents assisted in designing her special coat of arms.

Her comfort ship flew a flag with her coat of arms upon it.

Chapter Six

The fighting ships

King Jeffrey was out walking on the shoreline.

He walked up on Angelica and Heather.

He asked the girls, "what are the two of you doing on this beautiful day?"

Angelica answered, "we are on our way to my ship. We are going to travel out to sea for a short journey."

King Jeffrey looked very serious as he told her; "I wish you would be more cautious."

Angelica replied, "oh father I have my two warriors by my side. You know how well I use my sword. Do not be troubled for our safety."

King Jeffrey looked at his guards and told them, stay with Angelica.

Angelica reached out placed her hands on her father's shoulders. She kissed him on his cheek and said, "I love you also father. But I need to get on my way."

King Jeffrey realized Angelica was not going to stay where he could keep watch over her.

He felt tremendous concern for Angelica and Heather's safety.

He spoke with Queen Jasmine of his concerns. He told her, "I feel I need to get some battleships designed and warriors trained to command them."

She answered, "you are her father. Do what you feel correct. I stand with you concerning this. I think you are wise in your concern. She is a headstrong girl."

King Jeffrey began planning a better plan for the future.

He immediately spoke with the shipbuilders. The ships needed to be reinforced, with cannons and speed.

He knew the warriors needed training in battle upon the sea.

He had the head warrior brought before him and Queen Jasmine.

The head warrior arrived and bowed himself.

He told the head warrior to arise.

The head warrior asked, "what may I do for you, my king?"

King Jeffrey answered him, "I have concerns about the warriors getting trained in both land and sea battles."

"I am having some of our ships turned into fighting ships built for battle. Other ships built new to withstand and fight on the seas."

Together they made plans for the training to begin immediately.

King Jeffrey had the shipbuilders draw up and start building fighting ships.

Angelica could not resist being in the middle of the ship plans. She was fascinated with the cannons and training.

The fighting ships were to be built for high speed. The ships were also to maneuver quickly.

Before King Jeffrey's plans could be accomplished, Angelica's comfort ship was finished.

It was a day filled with the feelings of joy. Today the wind and sea are right to try out the new comfort ship.

Heather also enjoyed the open seas and found herself attracted to one of their new guards.

Angelica knew Heather's feelings smiled as she watched Heather glance over at the guard in a pure shy manner.

The girls giggled and teased each other.

Angelica and Heather left on Angelica's ship.

She was setting her course and steering her ship.

Heather stood by Angelica's side, smiling.

Angelica's long red hair was slightly blowing in the wind.

Heather and the guard kept looking over at each other.

The guard winked at Heather and Angelica laughed.

Heather showed herself shy and blushed.

Such a beautiful journey until small puffs of smoke caught Angelica's attention.

Short sounds like thunder quickened Angelica's alertness and caution.

The sailor on watch shouted, "turn away Princess Angelica. An intense battle takes place ahead of us between ships."

Angelica shouted, "what banner do they fly?"

The sailor on watch shouted back, "one banner is pirate. The other banner is of a kingdom I do not recognize."

The head guard told the other guards, "be alert and quick to battle."

Angelica overheard the head guard and replied; "we cannot battle on this ship. For the first time in mine and your life, we will have to run from the battle."

The head guard replied, "true Princess Angelica. Your other guards and I are ready to defend what we must."

The kingdom fighting ship is moving fast and overtaking the pirate ship.

The captain of the pirate ship shouted to his men; "this ship is too strong for us. Head out to sea quick men."

The pirate ship is now on the run.

Not good for Angelica because the pirate ship was headed on the run towards her.

The sailor on watch shouted, "Princess the pirate ship is on the run from the other ship."

Angelica shouted back at him, "which course are they heading?"

The Sailor on watch shouted back, "steer away Princess. They are headed at us, full speed in the chase."

She told the head guard, "I cannot get out of their path quick enough."

Have the guard who flirted with Heather watch over her. He cares too much for her to allow harm to befall her."

The head guard brought over the warrior to secure Heather for safe keeping.

Angelica told him, "if we sink or they board us I command you to keep her safe at any cost."

The guard hurried over to get Heather. As the guard reached for Heather, she pulled away from him and screamed, "no I will not leave Princess Angelica's side. She saved my life. She is my friend even as a sister."

Angelica shouted, "please go with him my friend, for my peace of mind. I need my thoughts clear now."

Heather looked over at Angelica and said, "alright but be safe Princess."

The guard took Heather to a safer place on the ship.

Angelica shouted to the sailor on watch, "are we clearing their course any?"

The man on watch shouted back, "no Princess. They come at us still in full speed chase."

She said to the head guard; "I do not have the power they do. I cannot avoid them."

Angelica asked the head guard, "where are Jason and his humor when I now need something humorous?"

She added, "as soon as we can see them close, have the men make ready for the clash of ships. She added that includes you as well my friend."

The head guard replied, "Princess you know we cannot do that. We are sworn to guard you with our life."

The sailor on watch shouted, "Princess they are approaching us too close now."

Angelica shouted back, "come from there and brace yourself."

The captain of the kingdom ship saw Angelica's ship had no weapons for battle.

He shouted, "get the pirate ship into the battle. We must draw it from their current course. The ship it is heading toward has nothing to defend itself."

The pirate ship fired on Angelica. The first shot missed. The second hit.

The kingdom ship started fighting the pirate ship to distract it from Angelica's ship.

The pirate ship was hit. The hit wasn't sinking the ship but did do severe damage. So, the pirate ship fled only to sink further away at sea.

Angelica's ship was sinking fast.

She had already ordered the men to abandon ship.

The kingdom ship approached the wreckage and gathered all they could.

Angelica push through the men and with tears in her eyes fearfully looked for Heather.

The captain saw her going into a full panic. He rushed to assist her if necessary comfort her.

With everyone wrapped in blankets, she couldn't find or see Heather.

The captain of the ship saw Angelica's panic overtake her.

The captain reached out to Angelica. He gently embraced her as she started to cry.

She finally just stood trembling and shouted, "Heather, please I beg you to answer me. Do you live?"

Off to her right side, she heard, "Princess she is over here."

Angelica and the captain rushed over to Heather. They asked, "do you need medical care?"

Heather rose to embrace Angelica.

The captain of the ship looked over at Angelica. He asked her; "you are a Princess from which kingdom? I did not recognize the flag you flew."

Angelica answered, "I am a Princess of a kingdom that you are getting ready to return me to."

One of the ship's sailors smiled and said, "you are safe ladies. The captain is the King of the seas. He is an honorable king."

Angelica responded, "I do not believe that."

The captain told Angelica; "he tells the truth, Princess. I am known as the King of the seas."

The captain said, "you are wet, and the wind will chill you." He took a blanket and wrapped it around Angelica's shoulders.

The captain told Angelica, "Princess I am an honorable man. I will return you to your kingdom, but there is a king I must see to gain his alliance with me against the pirates."

Angelica looked serious at the captain and paused for a minute.

Angelica replied, "take me home, and I will seek aide for you from my father and mother."

The captain looked very serious at Angelica and said, "the pirate ships have harmed many innocent people. This is a vital matter, be honest Princess with what you say to me."

Angelica replied, "I know the importance of defeating the pirate ships."

The captain asked, "how far away is your kingdom?"

Angelica answered the captain, "not far. I will help you set a course for my kingdom."

The captain told her, "you handled your ship and its crew well, with skill under the circumstances."

"Twenty-five was on your ship, twenty-five survived."

Chapter Seven

The Alliance

Angelica helped the captain set a course for her kingdom.

She exchanged her regal attitude for a woman of a kind compassionate heart. She went about the ship helping care for the wounded. Her soft words of encouragement eased their pain.

The captain watched Angelica's acts of compassion and smiled.

The captain said, "now her actions and words show her true heart. I see the beauty inside her God is pleased with."

His head warrior who is also his close friend stood at the King's side. He stood watching her encouraging, binding the wounds.

He looked serious at his king. He asked, "am I wrong or is this the dream you had?"

The King answered, "yes today has been what I dreamed and told you. Her ship, the battle, all exact. She is the same woman I saw."

His guard said, "as I watched her board your ship I couldn't believe my eyes. She is exactly as you described her."

His head guard asked, "did your dreams take you beyond this time?"

The captain answered, "surely they will."

He laughed as he continued. "I am not sure if I dare sleep to see if my dreams go beyond now or never sleep again."

The captain added, "we will see where our destiny takes us from here."

They laughed together thinking about how destiny unfolded.

Everyone's needs were cared for by the captain and his crew. Now all is peaceful while most rested.

Angelica slowly walked over to the captain.

The captain looked over at her quiet for a couple of minutes.

His look made her very nervous.

She asked, "why are you looking at me and not speaking?"

He quickly responded, "I cannot answer you truthfully without you misunderstanding my intent."

She told him, "just answer me honestly."

He smiled as he looked at her.

He said, "alright Princess. When I looked over at you, I thought, how amazing you look under the stars and in the moonlight."

"Are you alright and your needs provided?"

She smiled and answered, "yes I am tired, but all is well with me. You must be needing rest also."

She asked, "I can stay the course, do you need me to take over so you can rest?"

He answered, "thank you for your kind offer. I often enjoy the nights on the sea."

"There also are pirates to watch approaching us."

The captain's ship arrived in Angelica's shoreline the following morning.

The captain looked over at Angelica and said to her, "Princess this is the kingdom I was going to seek help from."

Angelica looked at the captain laughing. She said, "like you're the king of the seas."

The captain asked, "why were you kind, now mean? You ought to say thank you for saving you and your crew."

Angelica replied, "I would not have been in need of saving if you had not chased a pirate ship to clash with me."

The captain of the ship replied, "Princess I did not do that with the intent of your ships harm or any other wicked reason."

"I will have one of my finest fighting ships given unto you to replace your loss."

The guards and sailors aided in getting the wounded to their homes.

The captain asked her, "may I clean up and change my garments before I go to your mother and father?"

She answered, "I sent word ahead by a guard and Heather. We will go on to the castle."

Before Angelica and the captain could reach the castle, they were met by King Jeffrey and myself.

King Jeffrey with tears in his eyes embraced her.

The captain and I walked on to the castle. We left Angelica and her father to talk alone about what happened.

While the captain was cleaning up, a delightful meal was prepared.

Angelica was seated with Queen Julia and King Charles.

She giggled as she told them, "there is something about the captain which I find myself drawn to him. I cannot explain it. I feel close to him even now."

She asked, "isn't that strange?"

Queen Julia looked at King Charles and smiled for they understood.

King Jeffrey requested the captain be seated at his table.

Everyone was seated when in walked the captain. The sailor captain now appeared regal. Upon his head, he wore a king's crown.

Angelica leaned over and whispered to King Charles, "look at that. I truly find him handsome, but he called himself King of the seas. Now look he wears a king's crown on his head."

"How can I be drawn to a handsome fool is beyond me."

King Charles and Queen Julia laughed for they knew who the captain was.

King William walked to their table on his way to Jasmine's table. He paused and acknowledged them.

He smiled at Angelica and said, "you look beautiful."

She replied, "at least what I wear is real."

He smiled at her and told her, "Princess that was not nice. What I wear is all real and mine. Any way you look beautiful, snippy but beautiful."

King William nodded at Queen Julia and King Charles.

He said, "it is my pleasure to see you."

Queen Julia smiled as she replied, "it is our pleasure to see you. We will speak with my granddaughter."

King William laughed finding it humorous. He replied, "it is alright. I find it all amusing. I saw and knew of her ways before we met."

Angelica looked puzzled asked, "what do you mean by that?"

King William amused with his secret answered, "I mean you no dishonor Princess. One day I will tell you of it."

He left to be seated.

King Charles laughed as he told her, "Princess he is a true King. He is King William."

Angelica asked. "really he is? I feel embarrassed and foolish. Please tell me about him."

King Charles answered, "We knew his father before he died."

"He had ruled both a land kingdom and the islands."

"King William had only one brother. Both King William and his brother are very honorable and well-trained kings."

Angelica excited looked over at him. She caught him looking at her.

He smiled and winked. He knew she was surprised by his crown.

Queen Julia said, "the firstborn son John reigns over the land kingdom, by rights."

"William is called the king of the seas because his kingdom is the islands, northwest of here."

Angelica looking at King William said, "that must be why I feel close to him is the seas."

King Charles continued, "I haven't seen them since their father's death."

King William bowed himself out of respect than sat next to King Jeffrey.

While King Charles talked to Angelica, King William sat at Queen Jasmine and King Jeffrey's table.

Queen Jasmine told King William; "we are thankful for your rescue of our daughter and those with her."

King Jeffrey said, "yes King William we do extend our gratitude."

"I was told by my daughter and Jason you seek our aide against some pirates."

Queen Jasmine asked, "What do you need for us to assist with?"

"Don't you have the backup of your brother's kingdom?"

King William answered, "that is why I seek your help. My brother, John's kingdom, was taken over by a pirate king."

Queen Jasmine said, "then you seek our aid to defeat the pirates and regain your brother's kingdom."

King William said "yes Queen I seek both. My brother did not look to the future in building armies for land and sea. I saw more unmarked ships in our waters. I went to John and told him of what I had seen."

"My brother was concerned about the cost of building up such armies. The cost of building any number of fighting ships was not reasonable to him."

"The only way I was able to withstand the attacks is I felt the cost justified. My fighting ships saved my kingdom."

King Jeffrey told King William, "I have felt concerned about needing fighting ships. I had our head warrior set up training an army for our ships."

King William replied, "if you help me with defeating these pirates I vow to help make ready your fighting ships and warriors."

Queen Jasmine said, "that is a tremendous exchange. One I can agree with."

King William said, "these pirates must be defeated, or none of our kingdoms are safe."

Angelica watched and listened to King William.

She asked King Charles, "do you know if King William has a wife and children?"

King Charles smiled, winked at Queen Julia and answered, "I haven't heard of any. It has been a long time since I last saw him."

Queen Julia told her, "even involved with the serious conversation; you draw his attention. He appears to be attracted to you also."

Angelica smiled as she said, "now that is interesting for sure. I hope so."

Queen Jasmine told King William, "A wicked king once ruled over this kingdom. King Jabel traded with pirates. After we regained my father's kingdom from Jabel, we have been fortunate that they feared to return."

Queen Jasmine added, "the pirates feared to attack us after Jabel was defeated. I have been concerned new groups of pirates would try us."

"Like my husband, I feel it is time to do something to secure our kingdom's safety."

King William replied, "I know of your victory that regained this kingdom. My father told me of your legend."

"My father also told me you have the most fearless and well-trained warriors."

She said, "our warriors are as brave and trained as they were then."

King William continued, "My army is the most fearless and well trained on the seas. I seek your alliance to regain Johns' portion of the kingdom. You and I both know greed cannot be satisfied."

Queen Jasmine replied, "greed has no limit to its cravings. Power in the wrong hands is dangerous to the innocent. We have the power to spare the innocent, such sorrow. We rightfully cannot hold back."

King Williams said, "your armies could attack by land. The pirates will be distracted by that battle. You will have the advantage because the pirates are use to battling at sea. The land is not their natural place. My army will come in by sea."

"There are secret passages in the castle. John and I traveled through these passages as children. So, I know them well."

I thought about what he said, and I remembered my times in the passageways. I told them, "I have been in the passageways when I was a small child. I remember their entry. They are hidden entries to the castle from the water."

Queen Jasmine looked over at King Jeffrey.

He responded, "it is in your hands. I do feel such an alliance to our advantage. We either fight them separately or together. Together we have much greater power."

Queen Jasmine said, "we would join our alliance with you. This is not just your battle."

"We need to plan and draw out our battle strategies."

King Jeffrey replied, "yes, we do. I feel King William is correct. The pirate's weakest battle is on land, which is our strongest."

She replied, "It is best to distract them with what is strongest against them. The pirates are unlikely to know the secrets of the castle as boys who grew up there."

Queen Jasmine asked, "how long have the pirates had control of the castle?"

King William answered, "three weeks. Not long enough to know about the castles' secrets."

Queen Jasmine asked, "did your brother survive?"

King William took a deep breath then answered; "the messenger said my brother did not survive."

King Jeffrey replied, "after we finish eating we will call in those we need help to lead the attacks. Jason and King Charles's input will be of great value, as well. We must set up timely, coordinated attacks."

Queen Jasmine replied, "I agree with my husband, timing is crucial."

King Jeffrey asked the guard to request King Charles assistance.

King Charles gladly excepted.

I was already present.

Each of the kingdom head warriors was brought to be present for the plans.

Queen Jasmine asked, "do you have a map of the castle and the surrounding kingdom?"

King William answered, "yes I do."

He brought out a well-created map with fine, clear details.

Queen Jasmine had the map of her kingdom brought to her.

The two maps were laid together revealing the joined kingdoms.

He also brought a detail drawing of King John's castle. The secret passages faced the shoreline.

Access for my warriors will be easily accomplished.

King Charles agreed, "I was at the castle as your fathers guest several times."

"The amount of time to travel there on land is longer than by sea. I have traveled both by land and sea."

I asked, "what was your length of time from here to there?"

King Charles answered, "It was four days ride from here to that castle. We stopped to rest shortly three nights and resting our horses quite a few times. It is best to plan four days travel."

Queen Jasmine said, "before I went into battle with Jabel my father appeared to me in a dream. He told me, never enter a stronghold without first resting for mental and physical quickness."

King William replied, "I know that is great wisdom."

"I also believe in dreams and God's ways to give us direction in our sleep. I am careful always to pray only God reveal truth and instruction to me."

I added, "yes King James did believe and did instruct you several times in your sleep before battles."

King Charles said, "I could send for my kingdom warriors, but time seems to be a crucial factor here."

Queen Jasmine answered, "you are correct time is crucial. I know our army can easily win this victory."

Queen Julia and Angelica listened and watched with intense awareness.

Angelica struggled with not being in the middle of it all.

Queen Jasmine added, "I request your warriors, and some of ours remain here under your command King Charles."

King Jeffrey said, "yes that would be very important. We could battle with peace of mind knowing our family is safe here under your watch."

I added, "yes we will need you also to hold back Angelica, or she will be in the battle on a ship."

King William laughed. He said, "yes from what I have seen she has a fire in her soul."

I told him, "yes she does. Even as a small child she believed she was going to rule over the seas."

King William smiled with pleasure as he replied, "that very well may be her destiny."

Angelica looked over at Queen Julia and said, "it is not a maybe, I will rule over the seas."

King William was amused when he overheard her. He looked over at her and smiled.

King Charles told us, "it will be my honor to protect all here. I will do so with a clear mind and my life."

Queen Julia whispered to Angelica, "thank God he will remain instead of trying to ride with them."

Angelica upset looked over at her grandmother and said, "that is unfair to hold me here."

Queen Jasmine asked, "we must coordinate our attacks carefully. How long will it take you to arrive at the passageways from here?"

King William answered as he pointed on the map, "I can wait with my ships here. As you draw them out, I will enter here into the passageways."

Queen Jasmine responded, "that will be good. I feel the victory against the pirate king yours to win. It will show your power against the pirates to regain King Johns kingdom."

They marked out their journey and setting their place to battle.

The kingdoms' head warriors watched the plans on the map and listened closely.

All three kings and Queen Jasmine instructed their head warrior to gather their armies and provisions needed.

Queen Jasmine instructed her head warrior, "set aside a group of warriors to remain with King Charles and his guards."

King William replied, "my battleships are waiting for my command."

King Jeffrey added, "we will send provision to your ships ensuring you have all you need."

Queen Jasmine said, "send word to them. Two days we will ride out."

Everyone left after dinner to make sure all preparation was accomplished.

Angelica insisted on traveling with King William to his ship with supplies and instruction for his army.

King William said, "alright Princess but you will not be allowed on the ship when we go to fight."

Angelica answered, "I am brave. I have prayed over my sword never to harm the innocent. I also prayed my sword would be swift to destroy the evil."

King William responded, "Princess I do not keep you from the battle due to the feeling you lacked bravery or ability with your sword."

He added, "Princess my mind and heart would be distracted by you. That could truly prove dangerous."

His response made her happy.

She laughed as she replied, "that was a wonderful answer. I will not hide away on your ship. I do wish you to return safely. After all, you owe me a ship."

He laughed and replied, "yes I do owe you a ship. I will order one of my finest ships given to you."

On his ship, King William told the army to put away the provisions. He also instructed them to prepare for heavy battle with the pirates in two days they will sail.

It was an excellent time in the boat back to her castle.

King William could not keep from watching her nor his heart from being drawn to her.

Angelica shut her eyes, leaned back allowing her reddish-brown hair to blow free in the wind.

She told him, "as a small child I tried to capture the wind. I find now I enjoy the feeling the wind blowing through my hair and upon me. Not only the wind but I enjoy riding on the water."

He smiled with pleasure as he said, "I also enjoy the wind blowing through your hair and upon you. I find great pleasure in it."

She asked him, "is there a queen that rules at your side?"

He delighted in her question. He decided to not tell her yet of his dreams.

He answered, "no there isn't any that rules at my side. There will be a radiant queen at my side soon."

She looked sad.

She asked, "that is nice for you. Are you in love with her?"

He smiled and replied, "I am falling in love with her. I believe we are placed together by God."

She said, "does she enjoy riding with you on the seas?"

He answered, "yes. The sea knows we will have such a fire of love between us. The sea nor anything else can put out such love and passion."

He smiled as he added, "you are radiant in the sunlight."

She laughed then responded, "be careful or I will try to steal you from her."

He winked and said, "what a glorious challenge."

They reached the shore too soon.

He reached out to assist her off the boat. She smiled and took his hand.

He told her, "it has been a pleasure, Princess."

Dinner was being prepared at the castle.

They went on to their chambers to get ready for dinner.

It was a grand dinner full of love and laughter.

Angelica and King William could not take their eyes off each other.

The night before they were to ride out all the preparations were checked out. It is already.

Now for a good nights' rest.

King William quickly fell asleep. Dreams filled his night.

Angelica's face appeared than he saw her in battle with her sword.

He struggled even shouting out to her, "Princess be alert, the danger is sneaking up on you." In his sleep, he watched how hidden men appeared. The two men fought against her.

He shouted in terror, "God, I beg you to spare the woman you chose to reign by my side. Help her in battle. Make her alert and her sword quick with a powerful defense."

After he awoke he rushed to see Angelica.

She saw him first and began teasing him as soon as she saw him.

He told her, "I am glad to see you are well and busy being Princess Angelica."

She twirled around laughing as she continued teasing him.

He watched her with a joyful heart.

He said, "please Princess be alert very cautious while we are away, please."

She laughed and continued teasing him.

Queen Jasmine's army rode out the following morning.

Queen Jasmine rode in front with King Jeffrey to her right, and I was to her left.

King William set out to command the attack by sea. As he reached his shore boat, Angelica stopped him. He turned around when she spoke his name.

She kissed him. She laughed and said, "tell that woman who wants to reign at your side, I, Princess Angelica challenge her."

He laughed and replied, "Princess I think the challenge is mine. I feel you will prove to be a challenge to my peace of mind. We will find out if I am right about that feeling."

She asked him, "please allow me to go. I would fight bravely at your side."

He answered, "I promise I will return to you."

Angelica smiled and said, "I hold you to that as a King's honor to his words."

She laughed as she added, "See you soon King of the Seas."

She watched his ships set sail.

Unaware of her or the castle guards a member of a band of thieves also saw the armies leaving.

The man rushed to the others with news of what he saw.

The leader became excited by the thought of the castle left with the minimum guard.

The more he thought about it, the more he believed they could successfully overtake the castle.

One of his men said, "you do not know for sure how many remain on guard. Nor can you know how long the armies will be away."

The leader would not listen to the logic.

The band had a large number of men but feared to attack the castle until now.

They rode out towards the castle.

They spread out at the castle getting ready to attack it.

King Charles told Angelica and Heather, "Queen Julia and I will follow in a minute to walk with you by the shore."

The girls laughed as they walked out to wait.

A small group of the men heard the laughter advanced toward the girls.

King William appeared before Angelica in an vision.

He said, "Princess draw your sword. Be alert danger is approaching you quickly."

Angelica drew her sword as she did Heather was alerted and drew hers.

The girls saw the men in time.

They were ready to fight along with their two guards.

King Charles and Queen Julia at the door heard the commotion.

He quickly drew his sword and reached the girls with his guards.

King Charles attacked courageously back with his sword. He saw one reach the Queen.

He skillfully ended the man's attack from harming her.

The guards in and around the castle ended the fight of the rest.

King Charles laughed. He said, "I feel grand like a King again."

Queen Julia smiled at the girls and told him, "you truly show yourself brave in a kingly manner."

Angelica said, "thank God he sent a vision of King William to forewarn us of the danger."

Queen Julia looked serious over at King Charles.

She asked Angelica, "you saw a vision of King William warning you?"

Angelica answered, "yes he told me of the danger and to draw my sword quickly."

King Charles smiled. He said, "I am not surprised child. You captured his heart without any difficulty."

Angelica laughed. She said, "that is only fair since he captured mine."

King Charles added, "I feel like walking the shore in a kingly manner in honor of Queen Julia's statement concerning me."

Queen Julia smiled took his arm.

He strolled with regal confidence with a beautiful Queen upon his arm.

Queen Jasmine and her army were riding confident, strong. They traveled without any difficulty.

Men were sent quietly ahead clearing the way for the main battle.

They found only a small number of pirates until they reached closer to the castle.

The pirates were caught totally off guard. They proved to be weakest in a land battle.

The attacks were victorious.

Everything was working as planned.

King Williams army studied the map on the way to King John's castle. Each maneuver of attack carefully planned then memorized.

After our attack by land was waged and the pirates distracted, King William and his men secretly attacked within.

The secret passages from the sea was a great benefit to winning the victory.

King William found his brother in the passage barely alive.

He kneeled by his brother and told him, "I will return for you shortly after I defeat the pirate king."

"Hold strong brother for me please."

King John barely able to speak, whispered, "I will be safe."

He commanded some of the guards, "keep King John safe and cared for while I enter the castle."

He slightly looked in from the secret opening into the castle.

They had to pause until the chamber became clear briefly.

He gestured his men it was clear.

They made it into the castle undetected. They took the pirates by surprise.

The Pirate king faced King William. The fight was intense, but King William finished the pirate king's reign.

King John and his kingdom were regained.

King William quickly returned to King John in the passageway.

He told his brother, "John I have regained your castle. You must come through for me and your kingdom."

With great care he carefully lifted up his brother.

King William brought King John's almost lifeless body out of hiding in the secret passage.

King John shivered with serious chills and high fever.

Queen Jasmine saw King William kneeled by King John.

She hurried to King William and his brother.

With deep concern she asked, "does he still live?"

King William answered, "barely, he is serious. The wet cold has almost taken his life."

Queen Jasmine kneeled on the other side of King John.

She examined him to decide what his treatment should be."

King William asked, "can he be restored to good health again?"

Queen Jasmine answered, "I am not sure what is the truth to your question. It is in God's hands, more than mine."

She had special broths brewed from healing herbs prepared for King John.

She instructed two healers that rode with her to remain and care for King John.

She gave the healers step by step instructions for his care.

Queen Jasmine remained several days to oversee his recovery.

Once she saw he was going to be alright. She told King William, "We are now ready to return home unless you feel you need us here."

King Jeffrey added, "we will remain if we are needed but I feel we need to return to our family and kingdom."

King William and King John answered, "we will be fine now. Our sincere gratitude for all you have helped to bring forth."

After a night's rest and a good meal, Queen Jasmine and King Jeffrey with their army rode home.

King William remained at his brother's side until his brother was well and his castle, his kingdom was cleaned and secured.

He was able to regain his strength after many days of medical care.

King John again sat on his throne.

King William in gratitude honored his vow.

The guards announced, "King William has arrived and requested he be presented to the King and Queen."

They greeted him with respect and honor.

King Jeffrey asked, "it is an honor to see you again. Is all well?"

King William answered, "yes all is well. I returned to honor my vow to you."

Queen Jasmine replied, "you owe us nothing. We are thankful the kingdoms are without threat now."

King William said, "I brought two fighting ships. One ship for your builders to use as a pattern. I also brought some of my shipbuilders to assist yours."

"The second ship I promised Princess Angelica to replace her comfort ship."

Princess Angelica heard of his arrival she rushed to see him.

King William saw her hurrying to him. He smiled and told her, "be careful Princess, or I will feel you missed me."

She smiled with a flirty smile and gestures.

She replied, "I came to see if you honored your word to me."

He responded, "Princess I would give you several of my finest ships for a chance to see you again."

Her mother and father smiled with happiness.

He presented Angelica with a mighty battleship to replace her comfort ship.

She told her mother and father, "I must try out my new ship. King William must show me all I need to know."

King Jeffrey told her, "you must first ask King William if he desires to go."

Angelica answered, "oh he does desire to ride upon the seas."

King William replied, "it is alright. I know I need to get accustomed to her adventurous nature. With humorous gestures he added, she will challenge my peaceful nature."

Princess Angelica asked, "did you tell her what I said."

King William looked puzzled he asked, "who Princess?"

Princess Angelica looked sad as she answered, "you forgot. Does she sat at your side or ride the seas with you?"

He looked serious at her. He reached out and took her hand.

He answered, "Princess I am sorry, but I do not know who you are asking me about."

She sharply answered, "did what I said to you have so little value? The woman I challenged your heart for."

He looked at her with a smile.

He said, "Princess you are the only one with my heart."

"God revealed you to me as my soul mate before we met. You and you alone do I seek to reign at my side."

She jumped into his arms and said, "yes I will marry you right away."

He laughed, and so did her parents.

He said, "Princess I did not ask your parents or you yet."

King Jeffrey teasingly responded, "her mother did me the same way with trickery."

King William and Angelica married.

We decorated their wedding ship.

As they sailed away, we could see them embracing and waving.

Heather stayed at the castle but joined them many times for extensive visits.

Tricia, Angelica's sister, has grown so much. She is to be as her mother and sister. She was alright with the sword, but her heart is; set as a healer.

Tricia and Heather spend much of their time being taught in the healer's ways by both Queen Julia and Queen Jasmine.

Of course, they needed me to teach them wisdom and use of their sword.

King Jeffrey and I gave thanks to God when Queen Angelica gave birth to a son. His name is James II after Angelica's grandfather.

Queen Angelica gave birth to her second child, a daughter. Her name is Christina.

Chapter Eight

The next tale

As Jason looked up, he saw Angelica and a guard headed towards them.

Jason said, "well friends, I must go quickly. I feel I am facing difficult times with her expression and manner of her walk. Looks like my amusing wit and clever nature need to be superior at this time. I must make myself delightful."

These words turned the heads of the six men. Queen Angelica walked toward them radiant and regal before their eyes.

The six men rose to their feet, bowed their selves with a fist over their hearts.

Jason again walked among the six bowed men, three on each side.

Preston said, "bow Jason this is not your Queen."

Jason said, "even now I enjoy walking between you six. It does make me feel quite important. Yes, indeed it does."

Queen Angelica reached out to Jason. She took his hand in hers.

Queen Angelica asked, "Jason, why do you worry us so. You are supposed to be getting some rest."

Jason answered, "I was trying to."

He turned and pointed at the six men. He said, "they would not allow it."

He smiled with great joy.

Jason added, "my Queen they were so forceful wanting me to amuse them."

Jason smiled as he looked back at the highly nervous six young men.

Queen Angelica knew what Jason was doing played along with him.

Queen Angelica looked very serious and asked, "Jason should I have my guards correct them?"

Jason answered; "no because even under threat from them, I do so enjoy telling them my stories. It gives me great pleasure."

Queen Angelica replied, "they do keep you busy with something good. Maybe I could convince their head warrior to allow them to travel with you? We would always know where you were then."

The six men looked at each other in amazement.

Jason replied, "alright for I have not finished telling your story." Queen Angelica interrupted Jason. "She said you would have to save that for next time.

Next time I will have another story for you.

www.ingramcontent.com/pod-product-compliance
Lightning Source LLC
Chambersburg PA
CBHW070457130626
46555CB00003B/1045